Sto DISCARD

Writing and art by kids, for kids

Editor's Note

My first day of English class, sophomore year of high school, I walked into a classroom dark except for a single candle flickering on my teacher's desk. He stayed quiet, writing, as we all filtered into the room, nervously laughing and whispering to each other. Eventually, we took his cue and began to write too. This teacher, Mr. McGraw, soon became my favorite—because he gave us the freedom to explore language and literature in the ways that most inspired and invigorated us. In his class, I labored over poems, researched the Brontë sisters, and explored symbolism in *The Scarlet Letter*. I am still grateful for the space he gave me to learn and write how I wanted to.

Teachers have a huge impact on our lives— hopefully in positive ways but also, frequently and unfortunately, in negative ways. Most of the stories and poems in this issue take the classroom as setting and subject, examining the ways that teachers and schools influence who we are and what we do.

I hope you take this as an opportunity to reflect on the teachers who have nurtured your passions!

On the cover:
My Life
(Marker, colored pencil)
Yincheng Qian, 12
Dallas, TX

Operations
Jane Levi

Education & Projects
Sarah Ainsworth

Design
Joe Ewart

Stone Soup (ISSN 0094 579X) is published 11 times per year—monthly, with a combined July/ August summer issue. Copyright © 2020 by the Children's Art Foundation–Stone Soup Inc., a 501(c)(3) nonprofit organization located in Santa Cruz, California. All rights reserved.

Thirty-five percent of our subscription price is tax-deductible. Make a donation at Stonesoup. com/donate, and support us by choosing Children's Art Foundation as your Amazon Smile charity.

POSTMASTER: Send address changes to Stone Soup, 126 Otis Street, Santa Cruz, CA 95060. Periodicals postage paid at Santa Cruz, California, and additional offices.

Stone Soup is available in different formats to persons who have trouble seeing or reading the print or online editions. To request the braille edition from the National Library of Congress, call +1 800-424-8567. To request access to the audio edition via the National Federation of the Blind's NFB-NEWSLINE®, call +1 866-504-7300, or visit www.Nfbnewsline.org.

Submit your stories, poems, art, and letters to the editor via Stonesoup.submittable.com/ submit. Subscribe to the print and digital editions at Stonesoup.com. Email questions about your subscription to Subscriptions@ stonesoup.com. All other queries via email to Stonesoup@stonesoup.com.

Check us out on social media:

Stone Soup
Contents

Moods of the Week

By Carolyn Lu, 13
Katy, TX

On Sunday, I feel happy because I have nothing to do but play.
I sit by the computer and watch YouTube all day.
I send yellow balls flying with my white-and-purple racquet,
Then get out other strings—my violin from where I pack it.
I never feel stressed and always get a good rest.
I love Sundays, a day I have no tests.

On Monday, I am tired; it's the beginning of the week.
More geometry, science. US history makes me freak.
First though, at 7:00, is tennis practice in the morning—
"SWING MORE POWERFULLY!" is a constant warning.
My arm is so tired and all of my body wants to sleep.
But it's Monday and the whole school sounds like sheep.

On Tuesday, I feel depressed. I have homework that's due.
I get more homework, which I have no clue how to do.
To make matters worse, at 6:30 there's math club.
Then for dinner, I have to eat spicy sausage grub.
I go to my room and watch some online tutorials.
It's Tuesday, and I still can't understand factorials.

On Wednesday, I am free with nothing after school.
I eat M&M cookies, then splash into the pool.
My homework today is easy and quick,
So I go to HEB with dad, and strawberries I pick.
At home, with nothing to do, I don't get bossed around.
I love Wednesdays because I never break down.

On Thursday, I am tired; I have tennis once again.
I run around the green, returning balls and hoping I'll win.
I lose all my energy for the rest of the day.
I really don't want to write another essay.
Can't the teachers stop cramming in so many tests?
All I want on Thursdays is to Have. A. Rest.

On Friday, I feel okay—the tests are finally at their end.
The bell at 3:55 will make it start to feel like the weekend.
Before that, noodles, goldfish, and berries will get me through,
Just as long as no one packed me a cashew.
I trudge down the halls—this feeling only lasts for a while.
Fridays are okay because at least I will smile.

On Saturday, my mood changes, I end happy but start sad.
I start off with Chinese. Everything makes me look bad.
But after I finish, I am glad to have nothing to do.
Sometimes I go on the balcony and just look at the view.
I once again end up watching YouTube all day.
On Saturdays, I sometimes even go outside to play.

Cracks and Fissures (Canon PowerShot SX600)
Sage Millen, 12
Vancouver, Canada

The Serenity of the Simple Inquiry

Ms. Lavender asked a simple question—why can't Dawn answer it?

By Ella Yamamura, 12
Cary, NC

We sat in a circle, everybody facing my second-grade teacher, Ms. Lavender. She handed everyone a slip of paper.

"Now everybody," Ms. Lavender began, "I would like for you to answer the questions that I'll ask you—you may say them aloud if you wish, but you don't have to. Remember to write them down."

I took a slip of lined paper from Ms. Lavender's hand and selected a pencil before sitting back down.

Everyone else did the same. Ms. Lavender cleared her throat. "The first question is: what is your dream?" I pondered for a moment; nothing in particular came to my head. I bit my lip as my classmates shouted out answers:

"A scientist!"

"An author!"

"A zookeeper!"

"A doctor!"

"An artist!"

Ms. Lavender clapped her hands. "Wonderful, wonderful! Fabulous!"

"A human!"

I snorted and swatted the boy who had said that. "You're already one, goose-head."

"Now, now," Ms. Lavender cooed to me. "Joseph can be what he wants when he grows up."

I reluctantly bobbed my head up and down in a nod before sitting back down.

My teacher asked me again what I wanted to be when I grew up, her voice clearly laced with impatience. I tapped my pencil against my thigh. *Why was she so insistent? Weren't we a little too young to be thinking about that?*

I pondered, and thought, and wondered, and questioned myself in various ways.

"So," Ms. Lavender asked, "have you thought of what you want to be when you grow up?"

I shook my head and promptly answered no.

Ms. Lavender gave up.

It has been three years, and I still haven't come up with an answer to Ms. Lavender's wimpy question.

Seasons have passed: winter fell to cover the sky and ground like a veil, spring altogether changed the world, summer beat its hot sun against the crashing beach waves, and fall sent its fiery leaves traveling through the air. What do you want to be? The question rang in my head, sending waves of annoyance through me.

What do you want to be when you grow up?

Ever since I left second grade, I had tried avoiding Ms. Lavender as much as I could. All because of one skunk-snot question. I was a coward.

Then news came—news that changed half of my life in school. "Announcement: I would like your attention please," the principal said through the PA system. "We would like to let everyone know of Ms. Lavender's departure. We would like to see Joseph Millers and Dawn Cagonea in the principals' office."

I'd gulped as I heard my name being spoken. *Ms. Lavender's departure? What does that mean? Had Ms. Lavender left the school?*

———————————————

"I'm afraid Ms. Lavender has departed from us very recently," Ms. Cari, my principal, told us when we came through the doors. I sniffed but didn't say anything.

Joseph glared at me and smirked. "Has Ms. L moved?"

Ms. Cari put one hand on my left shoulder. I shifted uncomfortably.

"No," she told us. "I hate to tell you two, but you have once been in Ms. Lavender's class. And with that, I must let you know. Ms. Lavender, I'm afraid, has passed away due to a sudden particular illness."

I had never experienced anything that bad. Ms. Lavender had always creeped me out a little, but I wasn't ready for *that*. I laughed. "No, she hasn't. She's much too young."

Ms. Cari steadily met my eyes. I stared back up at her. I knew the principal was serious. I turned away.

"I want you two to think of something you can do for her. Something that can be buried with her at her funeral." Ms. Cari told us. "It can be anything. It's the least you can do."

"Okay," Joseph responded.

"Good," Ms. Cari said, smiling. "Dawn? What about you?"

I looked away in disgust. *How could anybody be smiling at this time? Do you smile right after you tell two fifth-graders that their old second-grade teacher died? No! This was ridiculous. That I knew.*

"Fine," I growled.

Joseph suddenly burst out laughing. I turned my murderous glare toward him, my scowl deepening. "I never noticed how funny you look when you scowl, Dawn!" He laughed for so long and so hard that by the time he stopped, his face was as red as a tomato.

"Are you okay?" I asked, watching as the color slowly darkened on his face.

"No kidding," Joseph gasped after the violent burst of laughter.

When the school bell rang, signaling the end of the day, I groped around my desk and drew out the old sheet of lined paper from second grade. It just sat there. On the top, the question stared back at me:

What do you want to be when you grow up?

I shook my head. After three years, I'd still ended up gazing at the same piece of paper.

I grabbed the sheet and raced toward my fifth-grade teacher. "Ms. Cari wanted Joseph and I to make something for Ms. Lavender," I explained. "Can you help me with this?"

My teacher nodded thoughtfully. "Dawn, which subject do you favor?" I blinked and answered, "Language arts. I'm interested in plants as well. Botany?"

Mrs. Bethany moved on. "Do your talents belong in art? P.E.? Music?"

I thought for a moment. "Art," I answered.

Mrs. Bethany looked at me closely, "Do you enjoy pouring out your thoughts on paper?"

I shuddered; all those years of staring at this one question made my stomach feel queasy. The thought of sitting in my chair, staring some more at a new blank piece of paper, wasn't enticing.

"No," I told my teacher hastily.

"What do you think?" Mrs. Bethany asked me, gesturing to the question.

I shook my head. "Mrs. Bethany, I don't know."

"'Be somebody who makes everybody feel like somebody,'" Mrs. Bethany suggested. "It's a quote."

No. I shook my head but immediately regretted it. I must have seemed like a bad person, rejecting a good suggestion like that.

Mrs. Bethany sighed. "Tell you what. You're too young to be thinking about your future, *worrying* about your future. Maybe you should take a break from this question."

I panicked. *I had to do something for Ms. Lavender quick! She couldn't wait forever.* Then I remembered: Ms. Lavender was dead. I nodded stiffly to my teacher.

"Thank you," I added absent-mindedly.

When I got home, I determinedly decided to fill the sheet in. But as I flopped down on my bed, the paper clipped in on a clipboard, I knew that I still didn't have an answer. But by the end of the day, I had filled it in. I puffed in relief. When I read it over again, I felt a boulder settle down in my stomach. This was not what I had been hoping for—not at all. It was filled with rows and rows of the same words.

What do you want to be when you grow up?

I don't know. Why don't I know? I don't know. Why is this question so hard to answer? I don't know. Why don't I know? I don't know. I don't know, I don't know, I don't know. I pondered, wondered, thought so hard for three years. At last I find the answer—perhaps this is the answer for now? Maybe? I don't know.

Dawn Cagonea

I felt like a vacuum cleaner had just sucked up my long-lost teddy bear or something. I was devastated.

I coughed, my pencil dropping from my hand. My handwriting hadn't changed in three years; what a surprise. I felt like a vacuum cleaner had just sucked up my long-lost teddy bear or something. I was devastated.

Why?

Because I couldn't answer a question from three years ago. *How smart am I?* Or, the more appropriate question: *how dumb am I?*

As I'd written on the paper, I don't know. But I had to change it. I didn't want everybody to see me in my fancy dress at the funeral and then read the dumb answer that I had written laid next to Ms. Lavender's body.

The funeral. Mom insisted I wear a long black dress with silver sequins and ruffles. But I wasn't going for it. So in the end, I wore a long-sleeved short dress with a silver necklace that sparkled in the moonlight. When we headed out the door, I grabbed the paper with my question and a new answer on it. I had slipped it in a sheet protector, ready to be laid alongside my teacher in her bed to heaven.

When I got in the car, I took the paper out of the sheet protector and smoothed its crinkles the best I could. I read it over again. It was much better than the answer I wrote when I was in the "I don't know" phase. I was happy that I actually had an answer. Sure, it was only a sentence long, but I couldn't think of anything else to write, so I had taken my teacher's suggestion.

What do you want to be when you grow up?

I want to be "somebody who makes everybody feel like somebody."

Quote by Brad Montague.

But then, as the car took off, I realized something: when Ms. Lavender asked us the question, she never got to ask us the other questions that she must have had stored up in her mind.

Underwater (iPhone XR)
Claire Lu, 13
Portola Valley, CA

Tales of Regret

A collection of enigmatic fables

By Analise Braddock, 8
Katonah, NY

Mouse Trouble

There were seventeen mice in a small and stiff classroom.

Every few seconds you heard a sneeze, and not one mouse really paid attention.

Instead, they passed notes and whispered.

One day, one mouse handed a crinkled paper to another mouse. The note read: "Yell as loud as you can, and I'll give you twenty bucks." The mouse flipped the scrap of paper over and wrote, "Yes." So, then the one mouse took a deep breath and screeched like 700 banshees.

She was sent to the principal's office as the other mouse laughed and said, "I'm not giving you the twenty bucks. Who are you kidding?!"

Vanessa's Letter

Vanessa was going to send her friend Clarice a letter. An important one.

She thought she knew Clarice's address and phone number, but she couldn't be sure.

She could ask her mom, but she was too comfy to move.

She wrote the address she thought was the correct address and sent it off.

Instead of Clarice's house, it got sent to people wearing belts and rags. A woman named Lagestry read the letter and smiled wickedly.

For she had a wicked plan.

The Moon, the Star, and the Sun

"I will destroy you," shouted the moon while chasing a tricky star. "Catch me if you can," snickered the star, running in a confusing circle away from the moon.

They did not know they were actually running around the sun.

The moon was big and wobbly and accidentally kicked the sun as it ran. The sun got really angry, and his face looked as if it were saying, "Don't mess with me, for I am the wrath of angels." The sun then roared and started after the moon. The sun was very quick and ran right into the moon. Then the moon ran right into the star. Soon they were all bruised and in a tangled mess.

Lana's Flying

Lana believed she could fly.

Every day she jumped off the diving board and flapped her hands after she jumped.

Every time she tried, she landed in the water in a belly flop.

She never quit.

Climbing Bark (Canon PowerShot G10)
Jeremy Nohrnberg, 10
Cambridge, MA

The Pages I Feared

After moving back to New York from Chile, where she spoke
Spanish in school, the narrator struggles to adjust

By Norah Grigoresco, 10
New York, NY

I started to pant as if I had run a mile, but I had only walked into a classroom. My breath came in quick, short gasps, and my mind was in a panicked rage, trying to grasp how I would survive this. Finally, Ms. Satenhart, my reading tutor, sat me down at a desk, and I watched in horror as she pulled out the thing that was bound to doom me from the start: a book.

When I was four years old, I moved to Chile and then moved back to NYC at six. I remember that tight feeling in my chest, excitement and anxiousness all swirling inside of me. But that feeling hadn't lasted long, for once school began, my hopes went from a soaring bird to a plunging fish, never meeting the bottom. In Chile, we had spoken Spanish, so on my first day, I couldn't even read a math problem. My cheeks were flushed red and my heart was squeezed tight in a bundle of shame as I mispronounced "thirty" for the fifth time.

Later in the year, my teacher had an announcement to make: "There will be reading tests in one week.

Read, read, read!" Her perfect, dirty-blonde hair and wide smile could make even the most stubborn birds sing. My mouth had fallen open as if to protest. But nothing came out, and my eyes had become glassy.

Over time I had come to admire my teacher, Ms. Wodlworth, and I hated to let her down with my failure. The first test came anyway, and only moving up one reading level had made my mouth feel dry, my nose runny, and my ears red. *I'm never going to make it.*

A month later, while sitting at my desk, I thought the torture had ended, those horrid pages hidden away, concealed forever. But I was wrong; they came back for me.

"It's okay for those of you who aren't happy with your reading progress so far," Ms. Wodlworth announced. My ears pricked up and my comfortable, plaid uniform didn't feel so comfy anymore. I felt itchy, how I always got before bad news.

"There will be reading tests in one month, so remember: read, read, read! Please go back to your books now. And remember your homework packet includes two weeks* of homework for the long weekend of Thanksgiving."

My eyes had started to sting, but I knew what to expect. Deep down inside, though, I felt a part of me that was getting tired of failing, tired of being pulled back, just like waves withdrawing empty-handed from the sand. It was a new feeling: determination.

"Time for bed. Go brush your teeth," my dad called.

"But Elias and I need something before we sleep," I complained.

My parents sighed in unison, "Water? A cookie? Just hurry. Then, in the morning, you complain about being tired."

"One story? Please?" My brother and I flashed our big puppy eyes.

"That's just another excuse not to sleep. You have school tomorrow," they reasoned.

"But I'm bored, and I can't fall asleep if I'm bored," I groaned.

"Good night," they called, and I fell back onto my bed. I blew my hair out of my face. Then, a brilliant idea struck me.

"No! Mom! Dad! Wouldn't it help me if you read me a story and helped me understand pro- pronunciation?" I said, practically begging.

"Do you really need help?" they asked.

"Yes."

Soon we were on the couch, my mom clutching a book in her hand called *The Lonely Little Monster*. In the story, the monster was scary, so other kids wouldn't play with him. But soon he tried his luck at friendship with a little girl. She realized he was nice, and the monster wasn't lonely anymore. After this struggle he had faced, he had finally succeeded.

"The end!"

As I dragged myself to my room, without any more excuses for not going to bed, I had started thinking. *What if the little monster was just like me? What if I—*

"Good night!"

"Don't go!" I jumped out of bed. Life in New York City had not been welcoming so far, and I clung onto any excuse to stay with the people who comforted me the most.

"What? Norah, you *need* to go to bed."

"But I can't sleep."

"Sleep is important. You don't grow if you don't sleep."

My brother claimed, "If I don't grow, it means I'll never grow old! I could be immortal! So I shouldn't sleep."

My parents laughed and said, "Love you."

"Ok. Good night," I sighed in defeat.

Once the lights shut off, it was just me and the sounds of New York. The sirens wailing with flashing blue and red lights, people honking, caught up in the web of traffic. I could even hear the faint tapping of high heels on the steel-hard concrete of the sidewalk.

I imagined the Little Monster, his green, shaggy fur framing his big, glossy brown eyes. A frown so small you would mistake it for an ant on his face. My thoughts resurfaced all at once, and I started to wonder, *Could I go through struggles just like this monster? Could I find the one light*

"Don't go!" I jumped out of bed. Life in New York City had not been welcoming so far, and I clung onto any excuse to stay with the people who comforted me the most.

to help me through this struggle? My ideas were muffled by my efforts to try to stifle a yawn. My weary eyes dragged down, yearning to sleep and find a quiet place. Slowly, my thoughts left the sound-filled streets to a place deep inside my head.

The next day at school, we were asked to do something that was almost impossible for me.

"Has everyone gotten an index card?" Ms. Wodlworth asked. We waited in silence until she decided to move on. "You will each get six minutes to write numbers one to 100 on the front side of the index card. Everyone ready?" She set the timer. "Go!"

One, two, three, four, five, six, seven, eight, nine, ten, eleven . . . I repeated in my head.

Two minutes later, my hand felt like it was burning off and I tried to push back the aching pain. Finally, I raised my head, my face beaming. I was done. I watched with eyes swimming in pride as the timer went down—three . . . two . . . one . . .

BEEP BEEP BEEP! The teacher paused the alarm and said, smiling, "Some of you are doing better than before! I want you to flip to the back of your index card and write the numbers again, but there is a challenge! You will have to write the numbers down from 100 backward. Ready, set, go!"

Oh no, I can't do it. I scribbled

down all the numbers that came to my head, and I was down to the last ten numbers when I heard that same fateful noise that had condemned all of my other peers last time and was now condemning me. The sharp, monotonous *BEEP!* bounced off the walls, and I cringed as my teacher said, "Pass your index cards to the center!"

I slowly passed mine to the center, but despite the disappointment from the second round, I congratulated myself. *Last week I hadn't known my numbers up to 50!* Suddenly, a thought flashed into my head: *I really am like the little monster! I learned how to count!* I looked around, and all my classmates at a level K in reading didn't scare me anymore. I stood up, my head held high, and walked down the hall. *If I can succeed in math, I can succeed in reading.* Excitement was bubbling inside of me, and I felt I was about to burst when we finally got outside for recess. It was a gray and cloudy day, but the beams shining off my face were all I needed.

A month later, I was sitting quietly in class when Ms. Satenhart strutted into the room. Her words came out in slow motion: "N-o-o-o-r-r-r-r-a-a-a-h?"

"Yes?" I hesitated. *Should I ask to go to the bathroom? Maybe I could avoid whatever mess she is calling me in for?*

"You'll need to come with me." She said this in a cheerful way as she stuck out her hand, motioning for me to take it. Once I had taken it, I felt the cool metal of the many rings on her hand. She had a small nose ring that shone against her pale face. Her dark eyes didn't match her bleached, whitish-yellow hair. As we walked out of the hallway, I noticed she had a habit of pulling on her red, woolen sweater. She looked down at her clipboard and then smiled up at me.

"Level B, huh? Are you ready to get better?" I wished that cheerful edge on her voice would disappear and get to the point. But I hadn't understood what she meant by "get better." *At what?* She had led me into a room, and I sat at one of the many empty desks dotting the dark-blue rug.

Finally, she reached down into a brown leather bag that seemed to have just been laying there and pulled out—as my heart dropped—a book. It was a slender, small testing book that, for the average person, would take three minutes to read. For me, it might take twenty.

"Am I supposed to read that?" I peered at the cover as she slid it toward me and took a seat across from me. The cover had a boy dressed in a blue baseball uniform, holding a bat in his hand, waiting for a baseball to strike at any time. The title was simple: *Bill's Magic Bat!* But I still wasn't ready. *Is this really what I practiced for?* I looked at Ms. Satenhart, but she motioned toward the book. I tried to grab it, but my hands were drenched in sweat, and the book kept slipping out of reach. Ms. Satenhart got impatient, took the book off the table,

and gently placed it into my arms. My knees started to shake, and I pinched myself to steady them. I pulled the book open and emitted a huge gasp. *So many words!*

"Can you read for me now?" smiled Ms. Satenhart.

"Okay." I flipped to the first page and slowly read, "Bill loved b-baseball?"

I looked up at Ms. Satenhart, but she only told me, "I don't know. You read it to me. Remember, you got this!" I looked back down and gulped.

I steadied myself and read in a faint whisper, "Bill loved baseball. But he had one secret to his success, his special baseball bat . . ."

Once I had finished the book, I looked up.

She scribbled down a few last notes, looked up, smiled, and said, "You pass! Let's go on to a level C book."

When I left the room, I was a level G. She told me she would test me again in two days because she was surprised with my progress. *Maybe the little monster was right after all.*

———————————————

A month later, all eyes were on me as I strutted down the hall. The pink paper crown that rested on my head read, "I'm a level Q!" This time I was top of my class.

Later, I was sitting in class when the teacher called me up and placed a shining medal around my neck. That, though, wasn't the award I'd been waiting for. As soon as it was time to go to the classroom library, I looked up at the teacher. I used to spend my time getting books from a kindergarten library, and the shame of it had borne down on me. I would hear snickers come from my class as I headed to the kindergarten classroom. Even worse, though, I heard the kindergarteners giggle. But now I was officially able to get books from my own first-grade class.

The teacher waved me on to the bins, and I felt my fingers tingle as I slid them across the rows of books. Finally, chapter books. Real first-grade books. I shifted over to a bin containing the biggest books. "Bin Level: Q." I looked around to see everyone else book-shopping on the lower levels.

A smile dominated my face as I chose my next book. *I can't believe it. I was so scared of . . . this?* I pulled out a book called *Dragon Boy*. *In the end it had all been so easy. Was this where practice could get me?* I dismissed my thoughts as I put *Dragon Boy* back and my eyes landed on a book nestled in the back of the bin. I grasped it with an eager hand and pulled out the dusty book, its cover only a glimpse of what awaited me inside on the pages. I blew on the cover, like they did in movies, and watched a billion dust particles fly off. The title read, *The Wolf Wilder*. I stared at the cover and, not even bothering to go to my desk, cracked the book open to the wonders inside.

Simple

By Adele Stamenov, 10
Bethel Park, PA

I sit down
Tired, anxious
But I can't relax
I stand up
Make some tea
Fresh and green
Add some milk
Puffy white clouds
Suspended in liquid
Floating in their little world
Take a sip
Warmth rushes through me
Things are better
Nothing complex
Everything is
Simple
Just me
And my tea

Happy Place (Acrylics)
Adele Stamenov, 10
Bethel Park, PA

Death by Kickball

Time slows to a crawl as Elenora wonders if she will make it out of a game of kickball alive

By Lucy Laird, 12
Pleasant Hill, IA

11:56, 11:57. I stared at my watch. The seconds ticked by oh so slowly. Seconds were suddenly minutes, and minutes were suddenly hours. At least, that's how it felt. My face broke out in a cold sweat, even though I hadn't moved a muscle. As soon as Coach Summit, the ruthless fiend, announced that we'd be playing kickball, I'd had a plan: station myself at the very back of the kicking line and pray for mercy.

It had to work. It *had* to work. But it didn't.

The line got smaller and smaller. Mia kicked, then Ben, then Jackson. Elliana kicked. Three people in front of me. Zero strikes. My heart rate quickened. Noah kicked.

I started to panic. How do you play kickball again? You kick, and then you run and try to catch the ball? No, that couldn't be right. Oh, my classmates are going to kill me! 11:59. C'mon, watch, C'MON! Move, clock, MOVE!

Rose kicked. I'm dead meat. As Oliver stepped up to kick, I saw my life flash before my eyes. What had I said to my family this morning? Did they know that I loved them?!

I remembered my fourth birthday when my mother baked me a beautiful rainbow cake. I was crazy about those little Jello cup things back then. She layered a normal cake with all of the Jello flavors she could find, making a culinary masterpiece. As I stood in that line, I saw her standing in the kitchen, carefully making the cake for me. So much love went into that cake. I never thanked her for it.

And what about all those hours my father spent reading to me before bed?! All that time, love, and effort, all for me, and I never thanked him. I would die without my parents knowing how grateful I was for them. It was too terrible to bear. I'm only eleven! That's too young to die!

"It's your turn to kick, Elenora."

I should have gotten someone to dictate my will before gym class!

No one was in front of me. I took a deep breath, gathered my remaining courage, and walked up to my fate worse than death. Twenty-nine eyes bored into me. My menacing classmates. I could practically taste their mad desire to win, could almost feel their wrath and infuriated screams. I was aware of every breath I took, every footstep. My heart

"I am a heroine!" I declared out loud, throwing my arms out into the air. I wanted to embrace the world, the whole beautiful world full of life and opportunity! "Freak," muttered someone.

was beating so loud, I'm sure my classmates heard it perfectly.

Life was such a beautiful thing, more beautiful than anyone could ever imagine! To gulp fresh air, to breathe, to go to sleep and to wake up to a new day! Oh, world, you're more amazing than anyone could ever realize! Oh, life is so beautiful and amazing, so unchanging, we can never understand it fully. How horrid that I should die right after I finally realized how amazing life really is! What a pity! What a waste!

It's always like this, I suppose. In all the novels I've ever read, the revelations always come before the cruel knock of death's hand on the door of life . . . Oh! How poetic! I'm turning into a real heroine!

"I am a heroine!" I declared out loud, throwing my arms out into the air. I wanted to embrace the world, the whole beautiful world full of life and opportunity!

"Freak," muttered someone.

I didn't care. No one knew what I was going through! No one knew how much I had matured in the last couple of minutes! My eyes were blind, but now they see!

I spun around in a full circle, arms outstretched, my hair floating rather enchantingly. It was a dull, dark black-ish color. Very unromantic. Well, not anymore.

I began to shout. "My hair is a rich ebony that frames my starry, violet eyes. Everyone who sees those eyes knows that there is a mystery behind them! For these are eyes which have seen both hardship and sorrow! Eyes that have had the bloom of youth brushed from them, to be replaced by wisdom! Eyes that—"

Coach Summit rudely interrupted my reverie with one of his famously feared "ahems." This "ahem" was not something to be ignored. Suddenly, all my delirium and delight seeped away like sand falling down an hourglass. The hourglass of my life, with every second my heart still beat, a grain of sand falling away, never to be retrieved.

Death was no longer romantic at all. All my happiness was gone. I closed my eyes tight and opened them again, hoping it would all be a bad dream, hoping it would go away, hoping that Mommy and Daddy could come to my rescue. When I was a young child, I thought my parents could do anything and save me from anyone. I knew better now. I had seen the world.

I closed my eyes a second time and saw it: My casket. White marble. I was being buried, to rot in the ground with worms and dirt . . .

No! I didn't want to die! I DIDN'T WANT TO DIE! I didn't want to leave everyone behind! I was only eleven, and there were so many things I hadn't done, that I'd never get the chance to do. How unfair that some get to live and prosper and that others must die at such a young age! How I had wasted my life so far!

But I couldn't ignore Coach

Summit's "ahem." I had to do what I had to do.

My legs propelled my feeble body to the plate. I decided right then and there that I wouldn't cry. I wasn't a heroine. I was just a silly little girl who couldn't play kickball. Still, I did have my dignity. It was all I had left, and I wasn't giving that, at least, to the ruthless hands of death.

Just as the pitcher readied to throw the ball, right before I died of fright, the most wonderful sound known to humankind rang through the gymnasium. The fates had been merciful. Some feelings cannot be described by mere words. It was the bell, signaling the start of lunch.

Laundry

By Zeke Braman, 9
Acton, MA

Standing
In my room
A feeling of impending doom
Comes slowly

Wondering
What path will I take
In this cruel world
Folding
Folding
Folding
The clothes rumpled
Like elephant skin
I sit down
Exhausted
Thinking
'How is this possibly going to end well?"

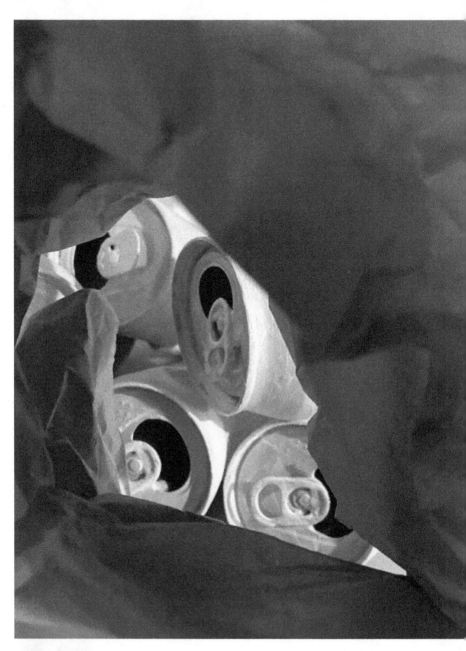

Through (Mixed media)
Jena Kim, 13
Seoul, South Korea

Meet Through News

Inspired by an unexpected discovery, Rosin decides to create her own newspaper

By Olivia Rhee, 9
North Bergen, NJ

The sun beat down on Rosin Molly Sully. The heat of the farm clouded over the barn like a blanket. Rosin's Rosin's uncle, Ronny, had been making hamburgers for the past thirty minutes. As Rosin hungrily got up from her work, she stared down at her red hands, which were covered in her sweat. The sour taste of lemons that she had eaten hours ago swept flavorfully in her mouth. The day was terrible so far. Minthe the dog didn't want to play, and Rosin's cousins were busy being mischievous.

Rosin walked with her cramped foot and aching back all the way to the small, ramshackle house. She loved exploring the old house. The bricks were dilapidated, and the front porch was covered in soft, green moss. The smell of cigarettes filled Rosin's nostrils as she crossed over to the front of the house. The hinges creaked as she opened the rusty old door. She went to the corner of the ramshackle house toward the rakes. The heat was making her pretty dizzy. She wanted to get out as soon as possible. But she didn't.

Out of curiosity, she grabbed a small rake that was leaning against the dusty wall and caused a chain reaction. Dust was everywhere as Rosin shook away the amount of rubble that had fallen too. She looked back at where the rakes had been when she saw a door that looked older than the house itself. Spiders crawled through the hole in the door. Ants crawled around the moss that was covering at least half the door. Little crayon drawings partly showed through. Beneath the door, a fallen chain lock looked like it had been there for decades, sinking into the ground.

Rosin opened the door, scattering ants and spiders. The lock made a terrible crashing sound as it went across the broken wooden floor. The dark room made it almost impossible to see. Then she saw something she had only ever used once, not even at home. There, behind the hidden door she'd found, was a ragged old pile of paper. Her family was ever so poor, and she hadn't started school yet, only because there wasn't enough money to go around. Her heart skipped a beat as she explored deeper through the thick darkness, having difficulty seeing. Suddenly, a small crunch came from under Rosin's foot. She looked down at the wooden floor and spotted some crumpled scraps of paper.

"Probably nothing," she said in a hoarse voice. "Just a ragged old page." But still, she cautiously picked it up and unfolded it. A small gasp escaped her mouth. She ran to the stack of paper she had seen earlier and picked it up along with the crumpled pages and brought both to the house, where Uncle Ronny was still cooking. It turned out that Rosin hadn't only found regular paper. She'd found fifty $100 bills.

Uncle Ronny served the plates and put two pieces of hamburger bread on everyone's plate.

"Get up, everyone! I set up a bar to choose whatever you want!"

Aunt Susan and Rosin's parents got up, smiling, and poured food onto their plates. Then Jaime and Rossie, Rosin's cousins, got up. Even Minthe got up to check out the kibble treats that were poured in her bowl next to the wooden cart—the so-called "bar." Rosin sat, though. She had something on her mind. She touched the money in her pocket and thought of the paper, which she'd hidden in her shoe closet. She thought of the many things that $5,000 could do for her. She could buy her own food and not eat from Uncle Ronny's bar. She could go to the mall and be part of the popular group in town by going; her life would be so much easier. Then, at that moment, a bright idea came to Rosin's head: She could go to school! She could be part of a better popular group, or even the best! Even the

thought of it made her squeal.

"Be quiet, you fool. Go get your food," said Jaime.

"Shut up!" Rosin retorted. Yet she got up and grabbed a plate to get some food from the bar, still thinking of the hundreds of opportunities she had with $5,000. When Uncle Ronny and Aunt Susan left with Jaime and Rossie, Rosin made sure no one was looking, and she got the paper out and went up to her pink bedroom, locking the doors. She set out the paper onto her bed and looked at the amount of paper she had.

"What could I do with this?" She thought out loud. She absentmindedly started doodling something she paid no attention to. She reviewed her choices of what to do with twelve stacks of fifty pieces of paper and $5,000. When boredom finally swept over her, she looked down at what her fingers were doing. Her dark-brown hair blew through the wind as Rosin rushed to a box of art supplies she used. She grabbed a black Sharpie and traced over her words in a neat print. She proudly looked up at her new creation:

Sully Times

Rosin left a note on one of her pages telling her parents she had found money. She only gave them half of it, though. She kept the other half in her unused piggy bank. Then, she organized her day. Morning Routine was the first thing for her to do, and the rest of what she would do was simple: work on *Sully Times*. A newspaper of her own would be amazing! She could get much more money! *Sully Times* could include major events in her town. She could add a crossword puzzle, games, ads, sudoku, and everything a child's newspaper could dream of. Rosin neatly started printing words:

This is a newspaper of fun, made by Rosin.

Then she ran off to her proud mother and father sitting at the small dinner table.

"How did you find it, sweetie? And where?" Rosin's mother asked her.

"I share the same question," said her dad. Rosin pondered this for a second. Should she reveal what she had found in that ramshackle house? The thought stayed in her head, and the family just sat there, peacefully eating.

"Well, I found it in the old house next door." Rosin whispered. Her parents nodded, though she could sense their greediness of wanting to search the house further for more. Everyone went back to their supper again, unaware of the tension building around them. Who in the room would have known that Rosin's news idea could make her family very poor, or rich.

———————————

RRRING! went the school bell. Students filed through the doors on the chilly September day. Rosin was in the midst of the students, but she wasn't talking like everyone else. She was looking around nervously. Posters plastered the brick walls, and a blue door was labeled "stairs." In front of the line of kids were two old teachers. One of the teachers'

name tags read "Ms. Karlio." She had wrinkles and a blue dress. She was a skinny but short woman with a beaded necklace. She was calling out the names of students who were in her class.

"Harmonica! Ellie! Aaron! Shawn! Rosin!" she called. Rosin went with the other students toward the wall and stood there absentmindedly. Her teacher seemed rough and older than most teachers she had seen. Rosin suddenly felt a pit in her stomach. She didn't want to go now. She saw her class move ahead but didn't go. She walked up to another, younger teacher and said she felt sick.

"Of course, honey. Would you like to go to the nurse?" the teacher asked.

"Yes, please," Rosin responded. "I would like that very much." She hurried over to the nurse with the teacher's guidance and lay in the cot, thinking how miserable school was already.

———————————

"Honey! John! Come down here!" Rosin's mother said. Rosin didn't hurry to come down. She tucked away her newspaper and walked downstairs. Her mother had a worried look on her face.

"I found out from your school that you were sick. Do you want to go to school?"

"Yes. No. I don't know!" Rosin yelled. She wanted to make her parents happy, but maybe she could go to a tutor. Her thoughts jumbled up when she realized something.

"Yes, Mom. Yes, I do. Bye!" Rosin hurriedly said. She sauntered off to her bedroom and remembered her idea: "Make the news and sell it for a fortune."

It was Monday at 3 p.m. Students were filing out of their classrooms to the yard to wait for their parents. Rosin followed them and took out a large stack of paper. It was neatly stapled together, and the front page read "Sully Times."

"News! News! Get your own copy! Twenty-five cents!" Rosin shouted. A few kids took out a quarter and got a copy. They ran off reading it. Rosin smiled at her work. Then she noticed a girl selling something. She had long blonde hair and a tie-dyed sweater. Her jeans and glasses matched perfectly. She was carrying a stack of paper too. A page got swept up in the wind and landed at Rosin's feet. It read, "Harmonica's Comic Corner."

Rosin stared at the work, outraged. Before she could stomp to the girl, she heard her mother calling. She picked up the other girl's paper and took her bag over to her mother, and they walked home.

"Are you ready, Rosin?" Rosin's mom called from the kitchen. Rosin was putting on her jeans when she remembered her newspaper. She swiftly buttoned her jeans and took out a copy. It was now a bit thicker than before. She smiled at it and recalled the girl selling comics. Rosin stomped down the stairs holding tons of her copies. Her father noticed it.

"Why such a heavy load? It's only your third day of school." Rosin didn't reply. She took a cup of cereal and a plastic bag. While stuffing all the papers in, she walked out the door and soon out of sight to school.

"Dismissed!" Ms. Karlio yelled in a hoarse voice. Rosin left as quickly as possible to the field. She saw the girl selling the comics and set up her own papers next to her. Rosin quickly glanced at the girl's work.

"Harmonica," Rosin muttered. She began selling copies but ignored Harmonica's smiles. Suddenly, Harmonica frowned.

"Are you mad at me or something?" she asked Rosin.

"Or something," muttered Rosin.

"Um, well, what about?" Harmonica asked. Rosin knew she couldn't hold in her feelings. She started breaking down about why she was mad, and how much it had taken her to just get an idea for a newspaper, and how Harmonica was stealing the spotlight.

"Sorry about that. I was making money for a charity. It's nothing to get mad about," Harmonica replied to Rosin.

"Sorry," Rosin said. Then she got an idea.

"Do you, well, want to make a school paper together? I could write, and you could draw."

"Sure!" Harmonica replied.

At that moment Harmonica had agreed, Rosin knew she had made a friend.

"Thank you."

Tree and Sky (Watercolors)
Djin Thornton, 10
Purdys, NY

Story

Asher writes about his difficulty finding a supportive, safe school environment

By Asher Jenvey, 10
Mountain View, CA

Second grade did not go well, but my story begins in first grade.

In first grade, my teacher was strict and made me think I could not read. I did not like reading to myself. I still don't like reading out loud. My friends from kindergarten the year before were not in my class. We grew apart. And my twin, Emmett, was in a class for special education that year. Emmett was literally unlearning stuff. The school said he was just stupid. When my parents told the school he had dyslexia, they said, "No, he is just stupid. That's why he's not in regular classes." My parents went to a man whose job was diagnosing people with dyslexia. He said that Emmett had dyslexia. After a long time arguing with the school, they gave up. So, in second grade he went to special school.

I felt upset and annoyed with the school. Second grade was not a good year for me. That year, I met Bully 1 and Bully 2. Bully 2 was Bully 1's lackey. Bully 1 was big with a little hair that was black on his head. Bully 2 was small and had dark hair. I met Bully 1 and thought he was a nice guy. He wasn't. He hurt me physically and

that hurt me mentally and I stopped making friends. Then I had no friends. I did not tell my parents because I felt it would not help.

But it continued. I became meaner after a month or so of this. Finally, I told my parents everything. My parents told the school, and the school did nothing. I was upset. I decided I needed to do something. After a day of thinking it over many times, I finally decided. I decided to waste the school water supply. I used the water fountain when I wasn't drinking anything. The school didn't seem to know anything was going on, but I kept doing it. Bully 1 was bored because I wasn't playing with him anymore. He decided to act as though he had given up his evil ways. I fell for it, so he beat me up. The principal was walking around nearby when they were beating me up and came close but did nothing.

That day, I decided I needed to do something big. So I clogged the sinks and toilets and left wet toilet paper on the ground. Everyone noticed that, and no one thought I did it. They blamed some other kid. I thought my school was going to be so unhappy.

Window of Black and White (Canon PowerShot G9 X)
Anya Geist, 13
Worcester, MA

They acted as though nothing had happened.

My school was still doing nothing about the bullies. I was still upset. My parents told me to stay home from school. So I stayed at home while the other kids were at school. My school said they would fix it.

I went back to school in December. I was at PE when the PE teacher told me to be in a group with Bully 1 and Bully 2.

I thought nothing would happen here, but I was very wrong. The bullies called me names and hurt me. I told my parents about PE that day. They were very upset. They told the school, "You didn't tell the PE teacher."

The school said, "We didn't think we needed to do that." I did not go to school the next day or the day after that. My parents argued with the school. In the end, in February, they decided to send me to a different school that was closer to our house.

The first day I went to the other school, I was scared and did not want to go. I wanted to stay home with my parents. My dad drove me to the school. I saw a lot of kids playing outside before the bell went off. My parents had told me what class I was in. It was Ms. Denue's class. I saw that the kids all looked nice enough, but you can't tell how nice people are from their looks. The bell rang and everyone lined up. I said bye to my dad and followed a line which my dad had told me to line up in. I followed the line to a classroom with a sign that said "19." I filed into the classroom and saw my teacher for the first time.

She was an older woman with long hair that was turning white. She said, "Please take your seats, class. We have a new student today."

Everyone stared at me. I was getting nervous. The teacher told me to come to the front of the class. I obeyed. In the front of class, my teacher said, "Can you please introduce yourself?"

I said, "I'm Asher."

Everyone said hi. They all introduced themselves. My teacher told me her name.

This was late second grade. I made friends soon after that with three kids. By late third grade, I started to think they were not nice and stopped hanging out with them. They were upset that I wasn't hanging out with them anymore and made a comic book that called me "toilet head." One of the kids outright lied about the comic book. The other two started crying and felt remorse and admitted to it when they were questioned by my mom. Even though this happened, third grade was one of my favorite years because I had a really good teacher named Ms. Casey.

After third grade, my parents made me go to a new school for fourth grade. The teacher was named Ms. Katrina. I made friends with two kids called Ronan and Calvin. I have much more in common with these friends than with the friends I had before. Ronan and Calvin like chess. We like to play similar games and talk about stuff I like to talk about. They are nice.

It was a good year, and now I am in fifth grade. My teacher is Ms. Sharp. Ronan and Calvin are still in my class. I think fifth grade will be a good year.

Splash of Sunlight (Canon EOS M50)
Paige Bean, 12
Leawood, KS

Cinka Times Two

Cinka's birthday wish is granted—in a very peculiar way

By Rose Fischer, 12
Colorado Springs, CO

"Happy birthday, Cinka!" said Cinka's teacher, Mrs. Reynolds. "I know it was your birthday yesterday, but it was Saturday, so the class will celebrate today. You're early as usual, so while I prepare, you can have some free time."

"Thanks!" replied Cinka.

She didn't feel like reading, so she got out a piece of paper and some colored pencils. The only thing she wanted as a birthday present was a dog, preferably a puppy, but her parents only said, "Maybe one day," or, "We'll think about it," whenever she asked. The best she could do was make pictures of her dream puppy and look at them a lot. She chose her favorite color of brown and started with a cute puppy face. She kept drawing and even drew a background with a dog bed and food and water bowls. Shadows make things look realistic, but when Cinka tried to draw them when she was younger, they just looked like blobs. Because of that, she left the shadows out.

Cinka took a step back from the table and looked at her picture. The tail of the puppy gave a little wag, but that must have been her seeing things. She rubbed her eyes and the shadows seemed to deepen. *Wait. Shadows?* Cinka hadn't even drawn shadows! She closed her eyes and counted to ten. That was better. Everything was back to normal. She started drawing an oak tree with spreading branches, and this time there were no weird shadows. The picture felt incomplete, so Cinka quickly made a line of ants before she went to the bathroom. When she got back, class had started.

"Put your drawings in your folder and get a dry-erase board before you join us," said Mrs. Reynolds.

As Cinka sat at her desk, she felt something wet near her ankle. When she looked down, her dream puppy was pawing at her leg. The puppy gave a little yip and tried to jump into her lap.

"Todd, stop making animal noises right now or I am going to have to send you to the principal's office," said Mrs. Reynolds.

"It wasn't me, honestly! I know I did it yesterday but—" protested Todd.

"GRRAF RAF RAF RA—"

Cinka covered the puppy's mouth and raised her hand.

"Can I go to the bathroom?" she squeaked and ran out of the

classroom with the puppy tucked in her arms before the teacher gave her permission.

After she locked herself in a stall, she sat the puppy on the floor and stared at it. On the one hand, she was elated that she finally had a pet, but on the other hand, she was worried: *Where had the puppy come from? And what was she going to do with it?* She couldn't bear to just leave it in the bathroom, but what would her teacher say? What would her *parents* say? Cinka checked her watch. It would seem suspicious if she hid any longer. She headed back to the classroom with the puppy and stuffed him in her jacket, which had been tied around her waist. When she got back to the classroom, she pretended she needed something in her backpack but instead zipped the puppy inside the bag with a gap for breathing. When she turned towards the board, she saw a little line of ants crawling up her teacher's leg.

"Uh, Mrs. Reynolds, there are some, uh—"

"EEK! ANTS!" shrieked Mrs. Reynolds. She started jumping up and down like there were ants in her pants—probably because there were. While Mrs. Reynolds was freaking out about the ants, Cinka took out her art folder. She had a sneaking suspicion that the puppy and the ants in real life might have something to do with the animals in her picture. Sure enough, when she opened her folder, the backgrounds were the same, but the animals were gone. It was as if the animals in her picture had walked right out of the picture and into the classroom.

After Mrs. Reynolds had finally gotten rid of the ants, it was already time for art. Cinka thought to herself that if she had to draw anything, she would leave out the animals just in case. When she arrived at the art room, the art teacher announced that today they were doing self-portraits. Cinka sat at her favorite seat and listened to the teacher talk about how to draw noses. They each had a mini mirror so they could look at themselves, but Cinka couldn't draw while looking at it. When she was done with the portrait, it was almost the end of class, so she quickly put it in the hand-in box without looking at it. After she cleaned up her supplies and was about to leave class, the teacher pulled her aside.

"Cinka, you've never done anything like this before, so I'm not angry at you. But why did you hand in a blank piece of paper?"

Cinka glanced around and saw *herself* walking out the door. She barely had time to process what she saw, and the teacher was waiting for her answer. Panicking, she came up with an excuse.

"Oh, that must have been Todd playing a prank!" she replied. "I saw him take a piece of paper out of the hand-in box and put a blank sheet in!"

The art teacher looked relieved. "Okay. I'll have a talk with Todd about that. Thanks for telling the truth," she said.

Cinka felt guilty because she was lying about Todd, but she couldn't think about that right now. She had no idea what she had seen, and the only explanation was that some other girl who looked kind of like her had walked out the door and Cinka had been so flustered that she thought it was herself. But as she got closer, she realized that the girl didn't look *kind* of like Cinka, she looked almost *exactly* like her. Wait—not almost—*exactly* like her.

Cinka's one thought at that moment was: *I knew it! The bubble monsters came, but they can't trick me!*

Cinka couldn't remember when or where she had heard about bubble monsters—or even if she'd heard of them at all. By now she thought that they were just something she had made up when she was very little, but if she were honest with herself, a tiny part of her still believed in them and was scared of them. Bubble monsters could make themselves look exactly like you, and then they ate you all up! The only way to defeat them was to look into their eyes and say "bubble." Cinka knew they couldn't be real, but right now she was so panicked that she wasn't thinking clearly. She ran up to the girl and looked straight into her eyes, still half expecting her to look different from the front.

"Bubble!" she whisper-yelled at the monster wearing her face, because she didn't want to attract attention. Surprisingly, the monster-that-looked-exactly-like-Cinka didn't disappear like it should have but jumped really high and then whirled around like it was looking for something.

"Wait, the bubble monsters are here?!" the monster cried. "Where are they?! Aaah—"

Cinka's mind raced. *Bubble monsters could not say "bubble," which meant . . .*

"Shhhh!" shushed Cinka. "I thought that you were a bubble monster. But if you aren't a bubble monster, then what are you? Wait, are you *me*?"

"It sure seems like we're the same person! We can't let anyone see us together. I'll hide somewhere and you stay in line."

Coming to an agreement with yourself was surprisingly easy.

"OK, but make sure you take the puppy. It's in my backpack next to my cubby. Wait for me in the library and we'll figure this out. While you're waiting, you can do my homework!"

"Okay!" agreed the other Cinka as she rushed off.

Original Cinka went to lunch with the rest of the class but left early to sneak into the library. The librarian was also on her lunch break, so she wasn't in the library. Cinka, wondering if she'd imagined the whole thing, was half expecting that the other Cinka wouldn't be there. But there she was.

"Hi! Did you finish the homework?" asked Cinka.

"Yep. And I was thinking . . . all the animals you drew came to life, and so did I—"

"So it must be all living things that I draw," the original Cinka finished. "We should probably do some kind of test just in case all of the animals and stuff were a coincidence."

"I think you should draw something small. If you draw a

dragon or something, who knows what could happen! It has to be something harmless. And it might not work if I draw it, since I'm technically a drawing," said Cinka 2.

Cinka 1 got out a piece of paper and drew a mouse head. She wasn't good at mouse bodies and just drew a dress to save time. She and Cinka 2 stared at the paper, hoping to see the transformation take place. They must have spaced out at some point, because when Cinka took a second look at the paper, the mouse had disappeared.

"Where did it go?" she said, jumping up and looking for it.

"There!" shouted Cinka 2. The mouse was running across the bookshelf with some pins and a pink ribbon and squeaking, "A dress for Cinderelly! A dress for Cinderelly!"

"You drew one of *Cinderella's* mice?" asked Cinka 2 in disbelief.

"Well, I didn't *mean* to," Cinka argued. "I just drew a dress, and I guess it looked like one of the mice from the movie. But that doesn't matter. We have to catch the mouse before someone sees it running around in clothes!"

Cinka 2 ran after the mouse, keeping track of it while Cinka 1 looked around, trying to find something to trap it with. Finally she found a big pitcher that the librarian usually filled with water and ran over to join Cinka 2. Cinka 2 put her hands around the mouse to keep it in one place while Cinka 1 put the pitcher down over it.

"Poor Cinderelly," squeaked the mouse.

"That mouse is way too concerned with Cinderella and not concerned enough about itself," said Cinka 1.

"But now we know that the animals definitely came from your drawings," said Cinka 2. "That means that the big question now is how they are coming to life."

"And why have they started doing it today?" added Cinka 1.

"Wait, do you remember our birthday wish yesterday?" they both asked each other at the same time. That made them both start laughing.

"It was to have amazing lifelike drawing skills and get a puppy!" said Cinka 1.

"Whoever grants birthday wishes must have taken that a bit too literally," said Cinka 2. "But at least you have the puppy."

"I have an idea of how to get rid of the animals!" said Cinka 1. "I need to draw a wish-granting creature and wish the drawings and my power away."

"But not the puppy!" said Cinka 2. "And make sure that you don't draw an evil sorcerer or genie or something because they might try to take over the world."

"How about the fairy godmother?" Cinka 1 suggested. "She seems pretty harmless."

"I know Cinderella is your—no, *our* favorite movie—but I don't really like it . . . whatever. But after this, don't draw anything else from Cinderella."

"Okay," replied Cinka 1. She got out another piece of paper and started drawing the fairy godmother. "There. Done. Now all we have to do is wait for her to come to life."

"I think there's no point trying to watch it happen," said Cinka 2. "It's like how a watched pot never boils—it's only going to happen when we aren't looking."

They both went to browse in the same section of the library. They kept picking the same books and bumping hands, and just as they were about to reach for another one, they heard a friendly voice say, "Now, I can't help you if you hide."

"It's the fairy godmother!" they both whispered at the same time. Cinka 1 slowly stepped out from behind the bookshelf with a mix of excitement and anxiety. Cinka 2 was right behind her.

"Oh, there you are!" said the fairy godmother. "What is it that you need?"

"Well," started Cinka 1.

"Oh no, don't tell me—you need tidier hair!"

"What?!" exclaimed Cinka 2.

"And you too!" said the fairy godmother. "Now where did I put that wand?! It must be somewhere. Aha! There it is!" The fairy godmother pulled her wand out of her hat, grandly cleared her throat, and started to sing:

Ohhhhhhhh, salagadoola,
menschica boola,
bibbidi bobbidi boo.
Put them together and what have you
got?
Bibbidi bobbidi boo!

As she sang, Cinka's hair twisted up and danced about to the movement of the fairy godmother's magic wand, as if the fairy godmother were conducting her hair. The books on the bookshelves joined, floating up in the air and dancing for another verse, and with the final "boo!" they fell lifeless on the floor. Cinka 1 looked at Cinka 2's hair and flinched.

"Uh, your hair looks like—"

"I know, I know. Your hair looks like a crazy version of Cinderella's hair too," said Cinka 2, rolling her eyes. "But we have other things to worry about. The fairy godmother still hasn't granted your wish. And I think she's going to do another spell!"

"Oh dear, What a mess! I think, to clean these messy shelves, I'll conjure up some—oh, where did I put that phonics book?" said the fairy godmother.

"Phonics book?" said Cinka 1, confused. She and Cinka 2 glanced at each other apprehensively.

"Yes, for some reason Cinderella thought that my rhymes weren't very good," the fairy godmother harrumphed. "So I got this phonics book to help. But I can rhyme fine by myself. Aha, here it is.

I think to clean up these messy shelves,
I'll conjure up some little elves.
Bibbidi, bobbidi, boo!

Six tiny elves appeared and started trying to pick up books that were three times their size.

"That's too slow," said the fairy godmother. "It's this phonics book that's messing me up. I'll have to try again. *Since you have made such a big mess . . .*"

"*We* made a mess?" said Cinka 1 indignantly.

The fairy godmother ignored her and continued: "*. . . you'll have to get a nice new dress!*" With that, Cinka 1's clothing turned into a simple pink princess dress. Cinka 2 snickered a little but stopped when Cinka 1 glared at her.

"Not enough, but I haven't finished the spell yet!" said the fairy godmother. She rapped her wand against her hand a few times, took a big breath, and sang, "*Bibbidi!*" The dress got a layer poofier and grew some ruffles. "*Bobbidi!*" It got even poofier and now had little sparkles around the edges. "*Boo!*" There was an explosion of lace and glitter, and Cinka 1 looked down to find herself wearing an elaborate, over-the-top Disney princess dress. She tried to imagine going back to class in this getup. Cinka 2 covered her mouth with her hands, but she couldn't stop herself from laughing this time.

"I don't see what's so funny," said the fairy godmother over Cinka 2's laughter. "It did work." And sure enough, the library was actually cleaner than it had been before.

"Excuse me!" said Cinka 1. "Can you just let me say something?"

"Of course!" said the fairy godmother, a little miffed. "I always let you say something. I never interrupt!"

The Cinkas rolled their eyes but told her a shortened version of the story, starting with the puppy.

"And then we drew you because you are so awesome at granting wishes. We knew you were the one for the job." Cinka didn't really think that, but a little flattery never hurt.

"Thank you, dear," said the fairy godmother. "That will be a complicated spell, but I can manage it. Just to be clear—you want me to get rid of all the animals you drew, and

myself, and also make this unusual power of yours go away. Is that all?"

"And make me disappear," added Cinka 2.

"What?" said Cinka 1.

"We're exactly the same," explained Cinka 2. "The fairy godmother will just be joining us back together again, not killing me—or you—or us . . . but you get the point, right?"

"I guess so," said Cinka 1 reluctantly. "I'll miss you a lot."

"Me too."

The fairy godmother cleared her throat. "Shall I do the spell now?"

"I, uh, well. I don't know," Cinka 1 said, suddenly uncertain. "I know that was the whole point of drawing you, but think about all the other things I could draw—like a genie who grants wishes, or a kitten that never gets bigger, or Peter Pan."

"But think about what could happen if you drew Peter Pan," said Cinka 2.

"You're right," agreed Cinka 1. "Wait, Fairy Godmother, could you leave the puppy out of the spell? Please?"

"All right," said the fairy godmother. "Oh, but like all dreams, your hair and dress won't last forever. They will disappear at the stroke of the teacher's pointing stick."

Cinka thought that was silly but was relieved the dress wouldn't be permanent.

"Goodbye," she said to Cinka 2. "I will really miss you."

"I'll miss you too," Cinka 2 replied. "And the puppy."

They both smiled.

The fairy godmother took a

deep breath and started the whole "*salagadoola, menchica boolla*" song. When she reached the last part, she sang:

> *But the thingamabob that does the job is bibbidi bobbidi boo!*

The fairy godmother, the mouse, and Cinka 2 all vanished, and Cinka 1 was alone in the library with the puppy, wearing her silly Cinderella-style dress. She sighed and picked up her backpack with the puppy in it. Cinka 2 had found some dog treats in the librarian's desk, and the puppy was still munching on them. She figured she could tuck her backpack just outside the classroom door so that she could keep half an eye on the puppy if need be. Hopefully the treats would keep him quiet.

She headed back to the classroom and wondered what in the world she would do when everyone saw her in this dress. Best case, she would be laughed at and remembered as the girl who wore a princess dress at school. Worst case, she would get in big trouble for coming in late wearing a costume. Luckily for her, all of her classmates were turned toward the board where Mrs. Reynolds was writing some equations. Now all Cinka had to do was get the teacher to wave her pointing stick, but it was too late. Mrs. Reynolds had picked up the chalk and put the stick on the desk closest to her—Todd's desk. Cinka watched him not-so-stealthily pick it

up and turn away from the board to present his prize to his classmates. When he saw her, his mouth dropped open in surprise.

"ABLUGUM!" he yelled with a grand gesture of the stick. The second the stick finished its arc, Cinka's dress vanished with a poof and her hair fell back into its normal half-ponytail. All of her classmates and Mrs. Reynolds turned towards Todd.

"I mean, look at her dress!" he corrected himself. Mrs. Reynolds narrowed her eyes.

"Todd, I don't know what you are yelling about, but if you disrupt the class one more time, I'll have a talk with your parents. Cinka? Where were you?"

"Um . . ."

"You know what? Never mind, just take your seat. But *no more disruptions*, do you hear me?"

"Yes, Mrs. Reynolds," they both chimed.

"Hi, Mom!" called Cinka. She had just gotten home and had decided that she might as well tell her parents about the puppy and get it over with.

"Hi, sweetie," said her mom. "How was school?"

"It was good. But I have to show you something." Cinka slowly took the puppy out of the backpack. It licked her face and then sniffed her mother. As if deciding by smell that she was worthy of attention, the puppy jumped onto her lap and curled up.

"What a cute puppy!" said her mother. She started petting it and called Cinka's father.

"What a cute puppy!" he echoed.

"So we can keep it?" asked Cinka.

"Of course!" said her mother. "Just one thing. Where did you find it?"

"It's a long story."

My Earliest Memory

By Audra Sanford, 8
Davenport, FL

My earliest memory
Is seeing my mom for the first time.
She held me lovingly.
It was warm and snug.
She tucked me in her lap,
Even when I cried.
I was very happy.
It was the happiest moment
Of my entire life.

The Dew Drop

By Esther Hay, 8
Ancaster, Canada

I wake up,
I walk out the door.
The dew smells like flowers.
As I walk,
I feel the morning mist brush against my tired face.
I see the daisies
so bright and blue.
As I touch them the dew falls off and onto my foot,
chilling me to the bone.
As I walk through the forest the dew falls off the trees
and keeps me cold.
As I walk home the trees shake in the breeze, all the dew falls
onto my face.
Now I am as cold as winter,
as cold as a polar bear.

Flower (iPhone 7)
Grace Williams, 13
Katonah, NY

HONOR ROLL

Welcome to the *Stone Soup* Honor Roll. Every month, we receive submissions from hundreds of kids from around the world. Unfortunately, we don't have space to publish all the great work we receive. We want to commend some of these talented writers and artists and encourage them to keep creating.

STORIES

Mayri Carsen, 10
Christabel Fernando, 11
Sage Hyatt, 11
Charlotte McAninch, 12
Ava Munt, 10
Jacob Su, 9
Anna Wetherell, 9

POETRY

Benjamin Ding, 9
Benny Dvorin, 9
Linus Fleischer-Graham, 12
Astrid Gothard, 13
Gideon Rose, 9
Mazzy Seja, 11

ART

Evie Humphris, 11
Dessie Mikels-Carrasco, 13
Li Rightmyer, 11
Ruby Xu, 10

BOOKS AND MAGAZINES IN THE *STONE SOUP* STORE

Stone Soup makes a great gift!

Look for our books and magazines in our online store, Stonesoupstore.com, or find them at Amazon and other booksellers.

Published on September 1, *Three Days till EOC* by Abhimanyu Sukhdial, the winning novella in our 2019 Book Contest. Hardback, 72 pages, $9.99.

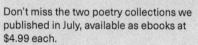

Don't miss the two poetry collections we published in July, available as ebooks at $4.99 each.

Current and back issues available, older issues at reduced prices!